W9-CLB-073

THE BOXCAR CHILDREN®

THE **MYSTERY** AT THE **BALLPARK**

Time to Read® is an early reader program designed to guide children to literacy success regardless of age or grade level. The program's three levels correspond to stages of reading readiness, making book selection straightforward, and assuring that when it's time for a child to read, the right book is waiting.

— Level —
1

Beginning to Read

- Large, simple type
- Basic vocabulary
- Word repetition
- Strong illustration support

— Level —
2

Reading with Help

- Short sentences
- Engaging stories
- Simple dialogue
- Illustration support

— Level —
3

Reading Independently

- Longer sentences
- Harder words
- Short paragraphs
- Increased story complexity

Library of Congress Cataloging-in-Publication data is on file with the publisher.

Copyright © 2023 by Albert Whitman & Company
First published in the United States of America
in 2023 by Albert Whitman & Company
ISBN 978-0-8075-0626-4 (hardcover)
ISBN 978-0-8075-0627-1 (ebook)

All rights reserved. No part of this book may be reproduced or transmitted in any
form or by any means, electronic or mechanical, including photocopying,
recording, or by any information storage and retrieval system,
without permission in writing from the publisher.

THE BOXCAR CHILDREN® is a registered trademark
of Albert Whitman & Company.

Printed in China
10 9 8 7 6 5 4 3 2 1 CJ 26 25 24 23 22

Cover and interior art by Liz Brizzi

Visit the Boxcar Children online at www.boxcarchildren.com.
For more information about Albert Whitman & Company,
visit our website at www.albertwhitman.com.

THE BOXCAR CHILDREN®

THE **MYSTERY** AT THE **BALLPARK**

Based on the book by
Gertrude Chandler Warner

Albert Whitman & Company
Chicago, Illinois

"I don't know," said Violet
Alden.
"I haven't played much
baseball."
A team was starting
in Greenfield.

Jessie wanted the Aldens
to join.
"Don't worry," Jessie said.
"We can learn together."
"Let's do it!" said Benny.
"It will be an adventure!"

Henry, Jessie, Violet, and Benny
loved adventures.
At one time they had even lived
in a boxcar in the forest.
It had been their home.

Then Grandfather found them.
Now they had a real home.
And they still had plenty
of adventures.

The Aldens agreed to give
baseball a try.
But at the field, there was
a problem.
Henry was too old to play.
Benny was too young!
Coach Warren had a plan.
Henry could be his assistant.

"What will I do?" Benny asked.

Coach Warren smiled.

"You can help Mr. Jackson.

He takes care of the equipment.

You will be our bat boy!"

"Really?" Benny asked.

"That's right!" said Coach Warren.

"After all, the game is

for everyone."

Jessie went into the field with
her lucky glove.
It was signed by her favorite
player.
She always played better
with it on.

Violet stayed at home plate for
batting practice.
She hadn't hit many baseballs.
And she was up next.
"This was my dad's bat,"
said her teammate Andy.
"It helps me when I'm nervous."
Violet smiled.
Maybe it could be her lucky
bat too.

After practice, Violet played
catch with a girl named Susan.
She told Violet how to hold
the ball.
She showed her how to step
into her throws.
Violet was happy to have such
good teammates.

Then a woman called out from
the parking lot.
"That's my aunt," Susan sighed.
"Sorry, I have to go."
Before Violet could thank
Susan for her help, she
was gone.

The next day, Benny watched
practice with Mr. Jackson.
"What position is Jessie
playing?" Benny asked.
"Shortstop," said Mr. Jackson.
"Jessie isn't short," Benny said.

Mr. Jackson chuckled.

"The shortstop stands between second base and third base. It takes a good athlete to play there."

"Jessie's a good player," said Benny.

"We'll see," said Mr. Jackson. "In my day only boys played baseball."

Benny frowned.

Wasn't the game for everyone? he thought.

At lunch, the Aldens went to get snacks.

A woman asked if practice was over.

It was Susan's aunt, Ms. Sealy. She wore nice clothes and shiny shoes.

"Sorry, we are just taking a break," said Jessie.

"You can come watch. Susan is doing really well."

Ms. Sealy grunted.

"You'll never see me on that dirt field.

If you ask me, baseball is a waste of time."
Ms. Sealy marched out.

After lunch, the Aldens were excited to get back to practice. But something was wrong in the dugout.

"My lucky bat is missing!" said Andy.

Jessie searched her bag. Her lucky glove was gone too!

Coach Warren crossed his arms. "I guess we have to end practice early," he said.

Even though practice was over,
Violet hoped to play catch
with Susan.
But Ms. Sealy called out from
the sidewalk.

"Sorry, time to go," Susan said. She hurried away with her aunt. As they went, Violet saw red dirt on Ms. Sealy's shiny shoes. Had she been on the field? Violet wondered.

A few days later, the team had
its first game.

They were playing the Pirates
from Silver City.

Benny knew just what the team
needed to change its bad luck.

"Every team needs a name,"
he said.

He pulled out his stuffed bear,
Stockings.

"Are we the Stockings?"
Jessie asked.

Benny shook his head.

"We are the Bears!" he said.

"Stockings is our mascot!"

The Bears got into the team
van to go to Silver City.
After a little while, Coach
Warren stopped the van.
He looked at the directions.
"No wonder I'm lost," he said.
"These aren't my directions!"

Violet turned to Jessie. "I think someone is trying to sabotage our team," she said. Jessie nodded. "The question is who?"

The Bears made it just in time.
The stands were full of family.

Mr. Jackson was in the dugout.
"I didn't think you would
come," he said. "I brought my
grandson to watch.
We were about to leave."
"We're here now," said Benny.
He waved to Mr. Jackson's
grandson.
"You can be assistant bat boy!"

During the game, the Bears'
bad luck continued.
Without his lucky bat,
Andy struck out.
Without her lucky glove,
Jessie made an error in the field.
The Bears lost 5–1.

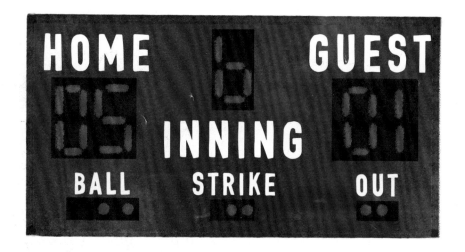

After the game, Benny said,
"I know why we lost.
Stockings is gone!"
"I'm beginning to think our
team is cursed," said Susan.

If the team was cursed,
Coach Warren didn't know it.
Over the next week, he worked
hard to help the Bears.
He gave Jessie his old glove
to use.
He found Andy the perfect bat
to replace his lucky one.

"Coach Warren has been so nice," Jessie said. "We should do something to thank him."

At the store, the children talked about who might be causing problems for the team.

"It might be Mr. Jackson," said Benny. "He said that in his day only boys played."

"Or Ms. Sealy," said Violet. "She doesn't seem very friendly."

Henry picked up a rare baseball card.

"That will make a good gift for Coach Warren," said Jessie.

Henry nodded.

But he also had another idea— one to help catch their culprit.

The next day, the Bears got
ready for their second game.
Henry told the team about the
gift for Coach Warren.
Everyone was excited to play
the Pirates again.

But in the dugout, Susan
looked sad.

Her aunt didn't want her to play.

Ms. Sealy thought Susan
should focus on her art.

"I'm an artist too," said Violet.

"If I can do both, so can you.

Let's go prove it!"

This time the game was close.
Jessie made a diving grab with
her new glove.
Andy hit a double with his
new bat.
Violet got her first hit!

In the last inning, Susan struck out three batters in a row. The Bears won!

After the game, the team
celebrated.
Henry kept his eye on the
team van.
That was where he'd put the
baseball card.

Everyone knew about the gift
except for Coach Warren.
All Henry had to do was
wait for…

"Ms. Sealy?" Henry said.
"Are you the culprit?"

"I saw your dirty shoes the other day," said Violet. "You snuck into the dugout and took the bat and glove, didn't you?"

"Did you change the directions too?" Jessie asked.

Ms. Sealy sighed and nodded.
"I didn't think Susan should be
playing," she said.
"I thought if I caused enough
trouble, she would quit."
"But she's good at baseball,"
said Violet. "And she likes it."
"I see that now," said Ms. Sealy.
"I owe you all a big apology."

With the culprit found, there
was just one question left.
"What about Stockings?"
Benny asked.
This time, Mr. Jackson
stepped up.
"I'm sorry," he said.
"My grandson loves dolls.
He grabbed it without
me noticing."
Benny hugged his bear.
"That's okay," he said.

"There's one more thing,"
said Mr. Jackson.
"I said that baseball was a boy's
game in the past.
But after seeing everyone play
so well, I know that Coach
Warren was right all along…"

"The game is for everyone."

Keep reading with The Boxcar Children®!

Henry, Jessie, Violet, and Benny used to live in a boxcar. Now they have adventures everywhere they go! Adapted from the beloved chapter book series, these early readers allow kids to begin reading with the stories that started it all.

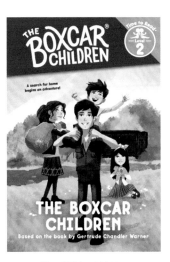  

HC 978-0-8075-0839-8 · US $12.99
PB 978-0-8075-0835-0 · US $4.99

HC 978-0-8075-7675-5 · US $12.99
PB 978-0-8075-7679-3 · US $4.99

HC 978-0-8075-9367-7 · US $12.99
PB 978-0-8075-9370-7 · US $4.99

MYSTERY RANCH

Based on the book by Gertrude Chandler Warner

HC 978-0-8075-5402-9 · US $12.99
PB 978-0-8075-5435-7 · US $4.99

MIKE'S MYSTERY

Based on the book by Gertrude Chandler Warner

HC 978-0-8075-5142-4 · US $12.99
PB 978-0-8075-5139-4 · US $4.99

BLUE BAY MYSTERY

Based on the book by Gertrude Chandler Warner

HC 978-0-8075-0795-7 · US $12.99
PB 978-0-8075-0800-8 · US $4.99

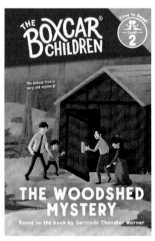

THE WOODSHED MYSTERY

Based on the book by Gertrude Chandler Warner

HC 978-0-8075-9210-6 · US $12.99
PB 978-0-8075-9216-8 · US $4.99

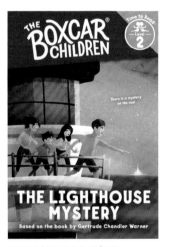

THE LIGHTHOUSE MYSTERY

Based on the book by Gertrude Chandler Warner

HC 978-0-8075-4548-5 · US $12.99
PB 978-0-8075-4552-2 · US $4.99

MOUNTAIN TOP MYSTERY

Based on the book by Gertrude Chandler Warner

HC 978-0-8075-5291-9 · US $12.99
PB 978-0-8075-5289-6 · US $4.99

SCHOOLHOUSE MYSTERY

Based on the book by Gertrude Chandler Warner

HC 978-0-8075-7261-0 · US $12.99
PB 978-0-8075-7259-7 · US $4.99

THE PIZZA MYSTERY

Based on the book by Gertrude Chandler Warner

HC 978-0-8075-6516-2 · US $12.99
PB 978-0-8075-6511-7 · US $4.99

MYSTERY BEHIND THE WALL

Based on the book by Gertrude Chandler Warner

HC 978-0-8075-5455-5 · US $12.99
PB 978-0-8075-5477-7 · US $4.99

THE SEA TURTLE MYSTERY

Based on the book by Gertrude Chandler Warner

HC 978-0-8075-0677-6 · US $12.99
PB 978-0-8075-0675-2 · US $4.99

THE MYSTERY OF THE MUMMY'S CURSE

Based on the book by Gertrude Chandler Warner

HC 978-0-8075-5499-9 · US $12.99
PB 978-0-8075-5492-0 · US $5.99

SNOWBOUND MYSTERY

Based on the book by Gertrude Chandler Warner

HC 978-0-8075-7510-9 · US $12.99
PB 978-0-8075-7452-2 · US $5.99

GERTRUDE CHANDLER WARNER discovered when she was teaching that many readers who like an exciting story could find no books that were both easy and fun to read. She decided to try to meet this need, and her first book, *The Boxcar Children*, quickly proved she had succeeded.

Miss Warner drew on her own experiences to write the mystery. As a child she spent hours watching trains go by on the tracks opposite her family home. She often dreamed about what it would be like to set up housekeeping in a caboose or freight car—the situation the Alden children find themselves in.

While the mystery element is central to each of Miss Warner's books, she never thought of them as strictly juvenile mysteries. She liked to stress the Aldens' independence and resourcefulness and their solid New England devotion to using up and making do. The Aldens go about most of their adventures with as little adult supervision as possible—something else that delights young readers.

Miss Warner lived in Putnam, Connecticut, until her death in 1979. During her lifetime, she received hundreds of letters from girls and boys telling her how much they liked her books.